HAPPY ZAPPA CAT

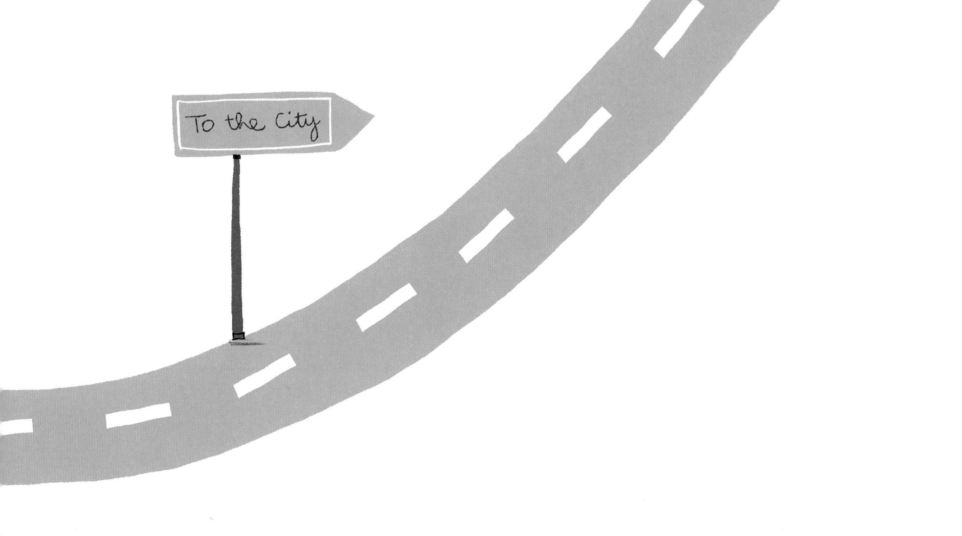

For Emily, with love
SW

For Clara and Fanette
MLH

SIMON AND SCHUSTER
First published in Great Britain in 2014
by Simon and Schuster UK Ltd
1st Floor, 222 Gray's Inn Road, London, WC1X 8HB
A CBS Company

Text copyright © 2014 Steve Webb
Illustrations copyright © 2014 Magali le Huche
The right of Steve Webb and Magali le Huche to be identified as
the author and illustrator of this work has been asserted by them
in accordance with the Copyright, Designs and Patents Act, 1988

A CIP catalogue record for this book is available
from the British Library upon request

978 0 85707 620 5 (HB)
978 0 85707 621 2 (PB)
978 0 85707 901 5 (eBook)
Printed in China
10 9 8 7 6 5 4 3 2 1

HAPPY ZAPPA CAT

TAXI

STEVE WEBB

Illustrated by
MAGALI LE HUCHE

SIMON AND SCHUSTER
London   New York   Sydney   Toronto   New Delhi

Cat Zappa, happy Zappa, happy Zappa cat,
zipping through the city in his city kitty cab.

'I am the happy Zappa,' sang the happy city cat.
'A zippy kitty city cat, my city cab is pretty fab.
Cat Zappa, happy Zappa, happy Zappa cat!'

MARKET

'I zip all over town, then back to the taxi queue.
Each time that I return, all the faces here are new.

Today there are some long necks,
some trunkeys and a snapper.
I wonder where they'll want to go?'
grinned happy Zappa.

Into happy Zappa's cab
the jungle buddies hurried.

He noticed in his mirror
that they looked a little worried.

'Don't you like the city?' he asked and turned his head.
The passengers all sighed, and this is what they said . . .

'We came to ride a train,
to walk the streets and see the sights.
    We came to catch a show
    and watch the pretty city lights!

We've seen the shops, the Museum
and the Gallery of Art.

We've been to Café Posh Nosh,
for their **famous treacle tart!'**

'Then, **whatever** is the matter?'
happy Zappa said, and smiled.

All the passengers together cried,

'We really miss the wild!'

'Please hurry to the airport,'
said the sad and lonely trunkeys.

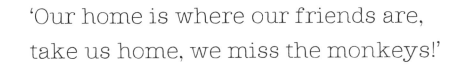

'Our home is where our friends are,
take us home, we miss the monkeys!'

Zipping through the city, on their way to catch a plane,
the animals began to smile, heading home again.

'I've never left the city,' said Zappa, thoughtfully.
'Maybe there's another world I really need to see?'

'Hop aboard this plane with us,'

happy Zappa's new friends cried.
'Come for an adventure,
come and try the wild!'

Happy Zappa left his cab and the city far behind,
and flew across the world, to see what he would find.

Over oceans, over mountains, over trees and waterfalls,
Zappa stared from the window at the wonder of it all.

They landed in the jungle
on a runway made of mud
with a rattle and a bump
in a wild neighbourhood.

They grabbed a jungle taxi and weaved through the trees.
A wild gorilla ride and a rather tight squeeze!

They danced through the jungle
and across the sunny plain.
They splashed through the swamp at night,
then did it all again!

Happy Zappa met the stripys,
the spotties and the sliders,

more snappers sleeping in the sun,
and great big hairy spiders.

Happy Zappa cat was happy,
at least for a little while.
But as the days went by,
he began to lose his smile.

His tail got tangled in the jungle
and the swamp was really smelly.

The sunny plains were way too hot,
he'd rather watch the telly!

All the others felt so happy back in their jungle home,
leaving only happy Zappa sitting sadly all alone.

'What's the matter happy Zappa?'
said the long necks and the trunkeys.

'Whatever is the matter?' asked a tree full of monkeys.

'I'll tell you what's the matter,' cat Zappa sobbed and said,
'I miss the pretty city lights, I miss my comfy bed.

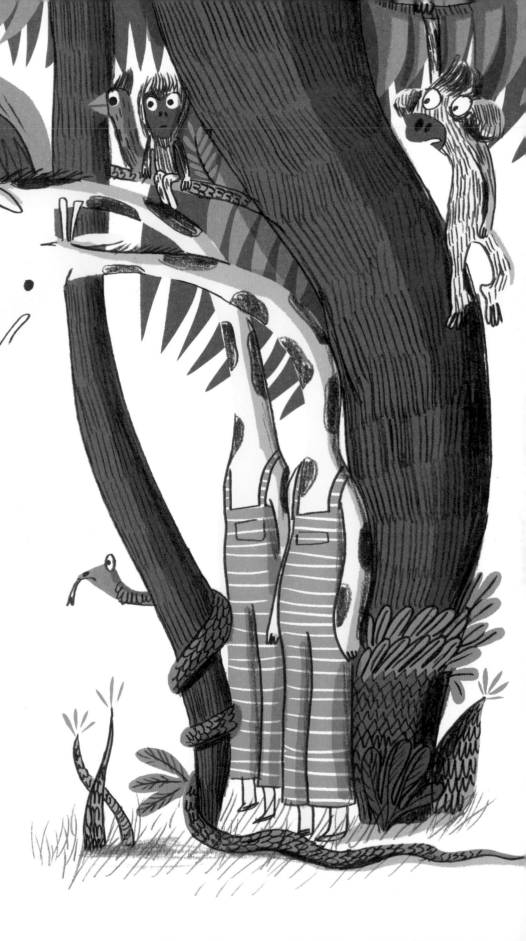

I miss the shops, the Museum
and the Gallery of Art.
I miss Café Posh Nosh,
and their famous treacle tart!

The wild is pretty perfect
for an adventure holiday,
but the city is the place for me,

I **have** to get away.'

GATE B

A DEPARTURES →

CUSTOMS

So the long necks and the snappers and the stripys and the trunkeys took Zappa to the airport and waved with all the monkeys.

'I'll send a postcard from the city. I'll miss you all so much.'
Happy Zappa waved goodbye and said he'd keep in touch.

A little later, from the window,
happy Zappa saw his cab.
And Zappa cat began to smile,
Zappa cat was back!

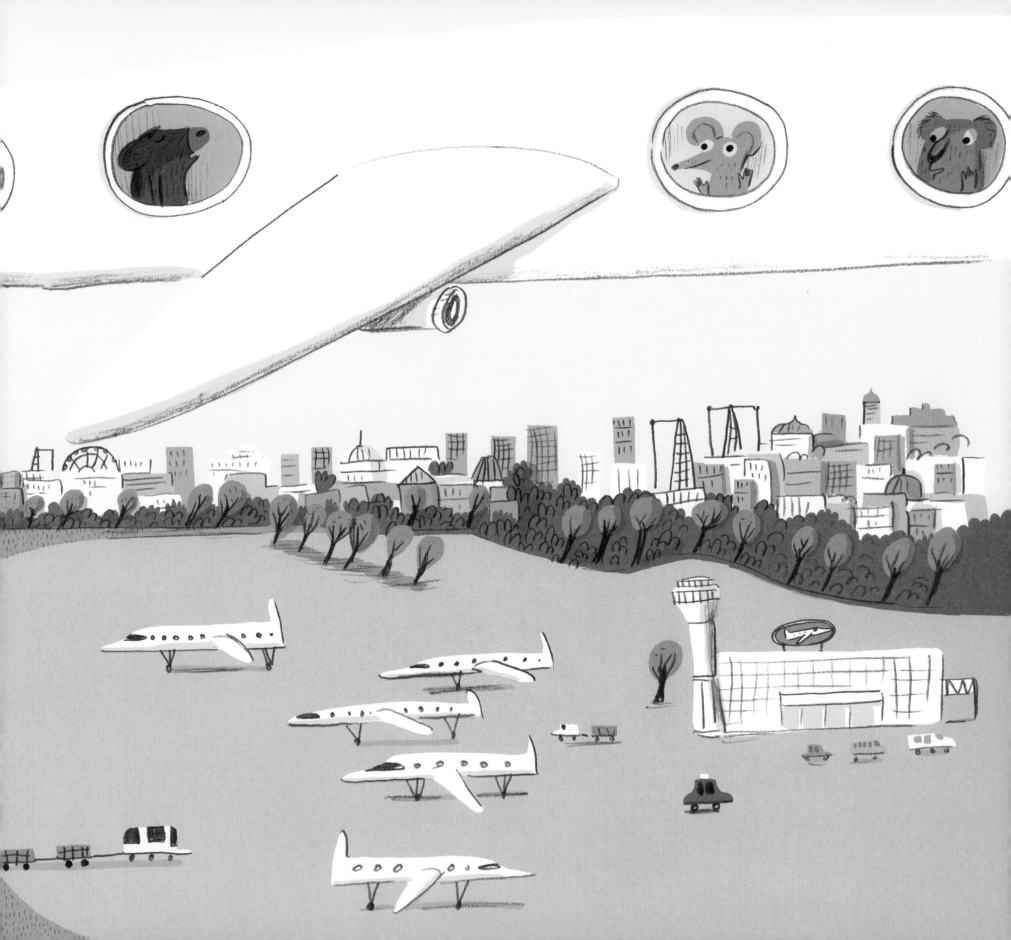

'I am the happy Zappa,' sang the happy city cat.
'Zipping through the city in my city kitty cab.

No matter where I wander, no matter where I roam,
I am the happy Zappa cat . . .

...there is no place like home.'

Cat Zappa,

happy Zappa,

HAPPY ZAPPA CAT!